The
EGG

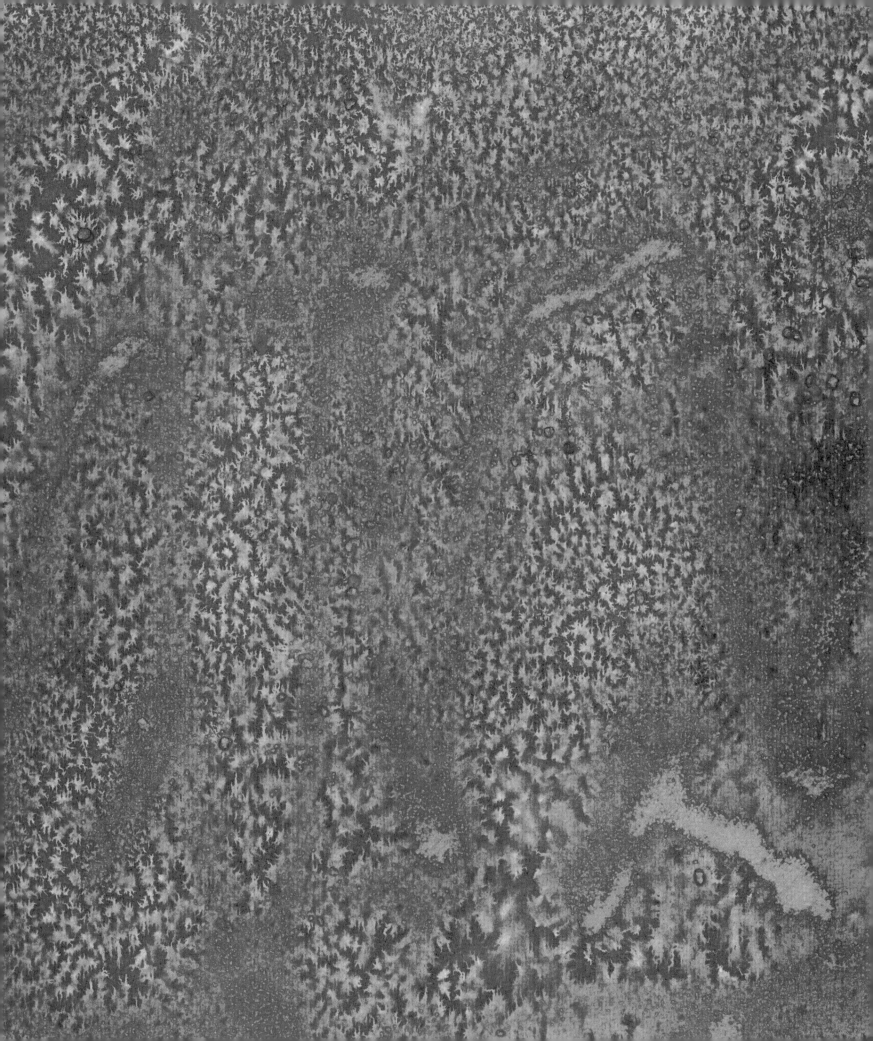

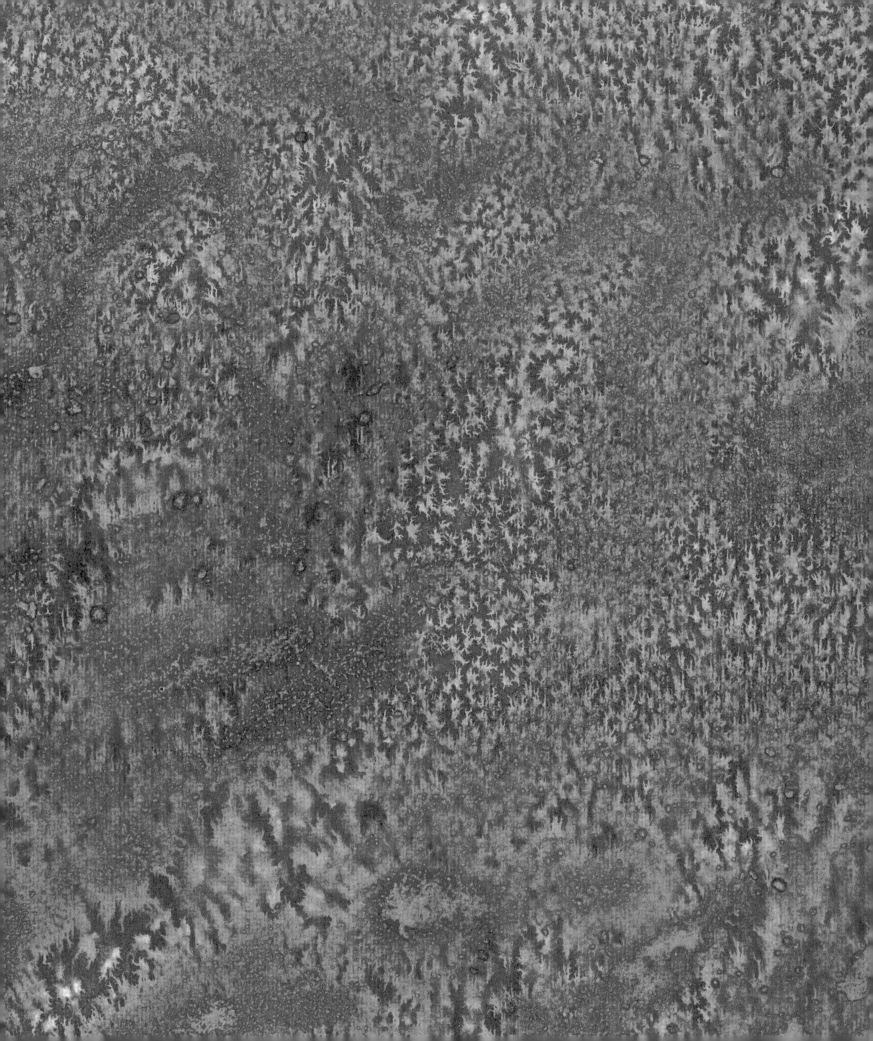

For Osky Bosky Boy (Oscar)—M.P.R.

PUFFIN BOOKS
Published by Penguin Group
Penguin Young Readers Group,
345 Hudson Street, New York, New York 10014, U.S.A.
Penguin Books Ltd, 80 Strand, London WC2R ORL, England
Penguin Books Australia Ltd, 250 Camberwell Road, Camberwell, Victoria 3124, Australia
Penguin Books Canada Ltd, 10 Alcorn Avenue, Toronto, Ontario, Canada M4V 3B2
Penguin Books (N.Z.) Ltd, 182-190 Wairau Road, Auckland 10, New Zealand

Published in Great Britain by Frances Lincoln Limited, 2000
First published in the United States of America by Phyllis Fogelman Books,
an imprint of Penguin Putnam Books for Young Readers, 2001
Published by Puffin Books, a division of Penguin Young Readers Group, 2004

5 7 9 10 8 6 4

Copyright © M. P. Robertson, 2000

Library of Congress Cataloging-in-Publication Data is available on request.

Puffin Books ISBN 0-14-240038-6

Printed in China

The EGG

M. P. Robertson

Puffin Books

George knew something wasn't right when he found more than he had bargained for under his mother's favorite chicken.

He moved the egg to the warmth
of his bedroom. For three days
and three nights he read the egg stories.

On the third night the egg started to rumble.

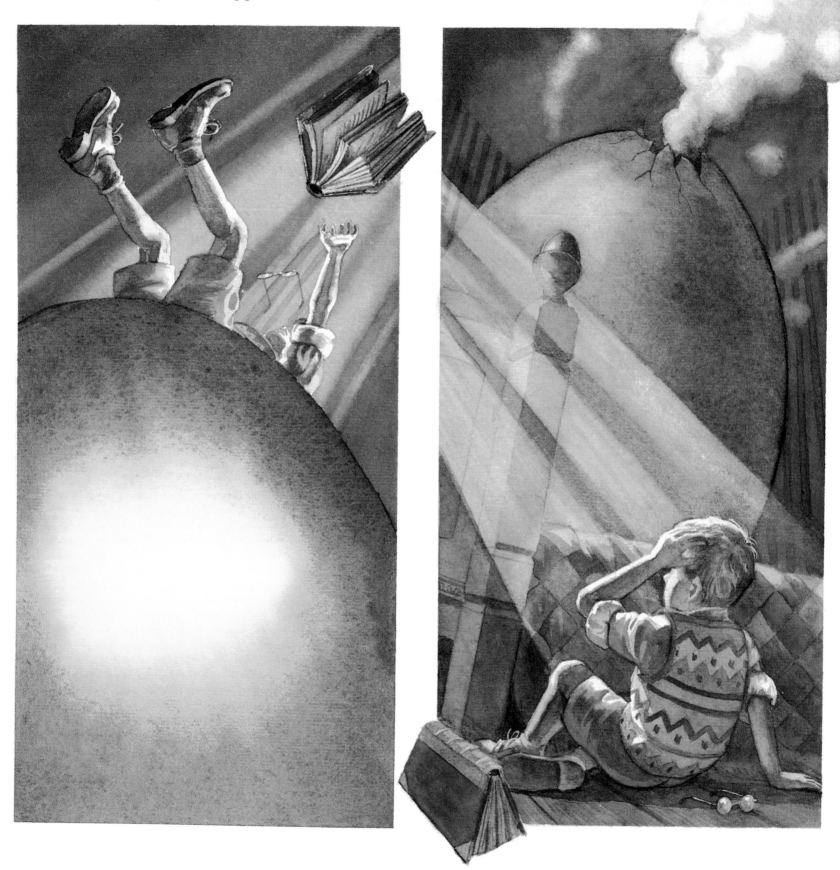

Something was hatching, and it definitely wasn't a chicken!

When the dragon saw George, it gave a chirrup of delight.

George didn't speak Dragon, but he knew exactly what the dragon had said:
"Mommy."

George had never been a mother before, but he knew that it was his motherly duty to teach the dragon dragony ways.

The first lesson he taught was *The Fine Art of Flying*.

The second lesson was *Fire and How to Breathe It.*

The third lesson was *How to Distress a Damsel*.

And the final lesson was *How to Defeat a Knight*.

Every evening, as all good mothers should, George read the dragon a bedtime story.

One night, as he read from a book of dragon tales, the dragon looked longingly at the pictures. A sizzling tear rolled down his scaly cheek.

The dragon was lonely. He was missing his own kind.

The next morning the dragon had gone.
George was very sad. He thought he
would never see his dragon again.

But seven nights later he was woken
by the beating of wings. Excitedly
he pulled back the curtains. There, perched in
the tree, was the dragon. George opened
the window and clambered onto his back.

They soared into the night,
chasing the moon around
the world, over oceans and
mountains and cities.

Faster and faster they went,
until they came to a place that
was neither North nor South,
East nor West.

They swooped down through the clouds into a cave that gaped like a dragon's jaws. This was the place where dragons lived.

The dragon gave a roar of delight. He was home at last.

Finally it was time for George to leave.
Up, up they flew, chasing sleep through the night,
until they could see his home below.

George hugged his dragon tight,
and the dragon gave a roar. George
didn't speak Dragon, but he knew
exactly what the dragon had said:

"Thank you."

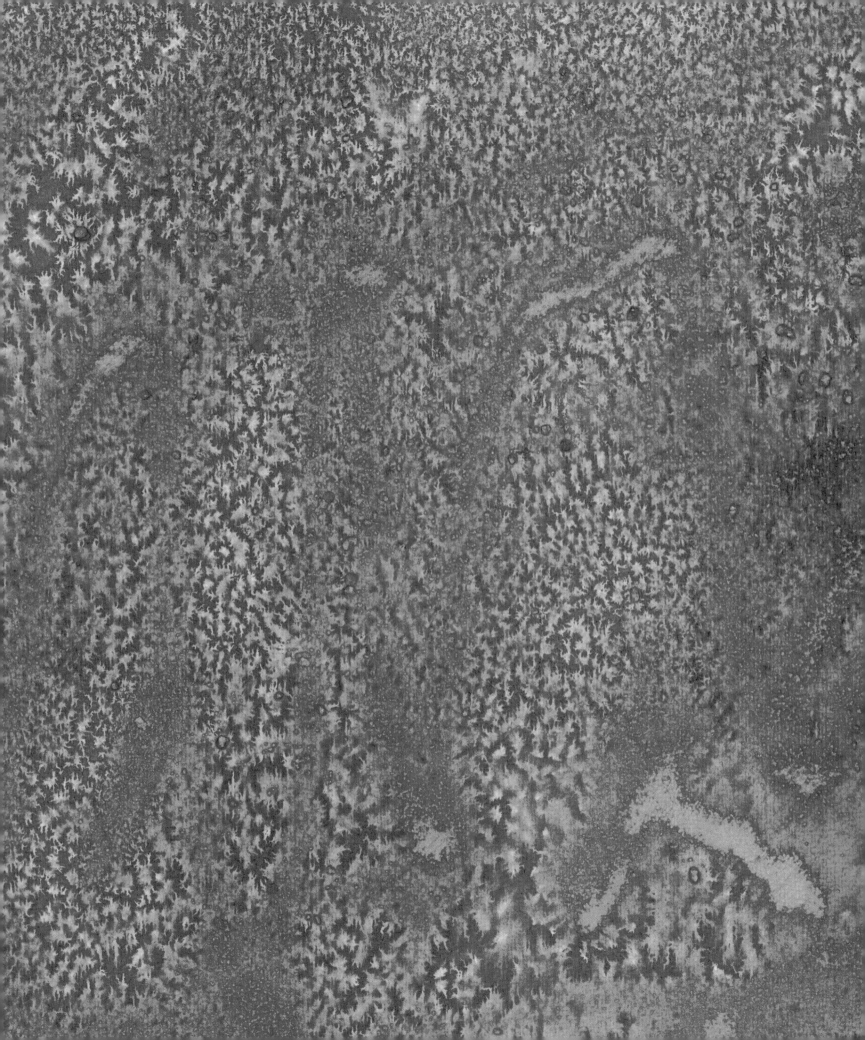

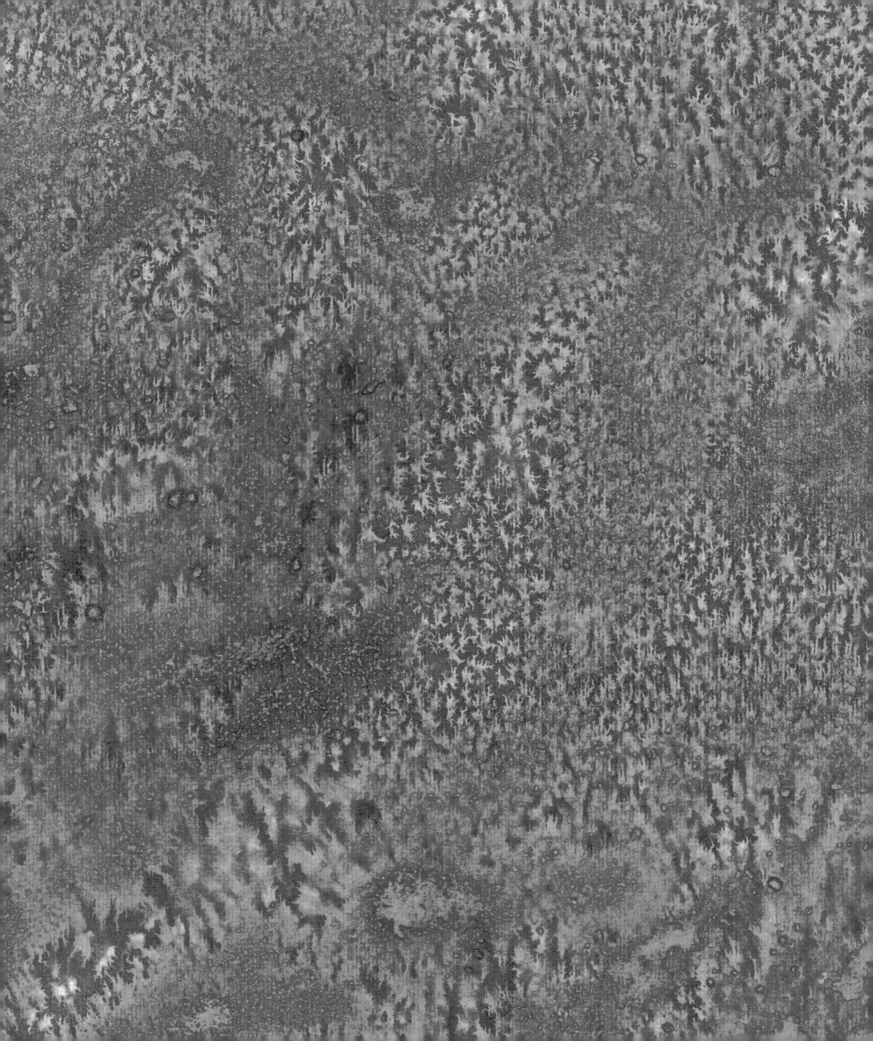